"We have a special visitor at the Ice Cream Shop this afternoon, girls," said Officer Grover Greenwood. "This is the mayor of Spring Grove, Harmon Waters."

"I've never met a real mayor before," said Ruthann. She and her little sister, Polly, were good friends of Officer Greenwood. They often ran into him at the Spring Grove Ice Cream Shop. Officer Greenwood was very fond of ice cream treats, particularly banana splits. He liked them almost as much as Ruthann and Polly did.

"It's an important job, being mayor," said Officer Greenwood. "The mayor of a town helps people to decide where the parks and schools should be. He also helps them decide how many police officers and fire fighters the town needs."

"And the people decide who will be mayor by having an election," said Mayor Waters. "Our next election will be held in just four weeks. Today I'm going around talking to the people of Spring Grove. I want to find out about their problems and about ways that I can help them if I'm re-elected."

The Mystery of
The Hidden Camera

by Dan Cohen + *Pictures by* George Overlie

CAROLRHODA BOOKS

MINNEAPOLIS, MINNESOTA U.S.A.

"Can you help me learn how to say . . . 'Ossifer' right?" asked Polly. Polly had a problem saying the word "Officer." Because of this, she had special permission to call Officer Greenwood by his first name.

"I could try," said Mayor Waters.

"I know a *real* problem that needs solving," said Ruthann. She glared at Polly. Sometimes a little sister could be so embarrassing. "I read in the paper about a man who wants to build a plant in Spring Grove that will cause a lot of pollution. If he gets his way, our air will be all dirty and our water won't be safe to drink."

"I think you mean Henry Simpson," said Mayor Waters. "I am not in favor of letting Mr. Simpson build his plant in Spring Grove. And the city does have the right to stop him.

If Mr. Simpson would agree to put an air-cleaning system and a system to cool and filter water in his plant, then it would be a different matter. But he says they cost too much money. That is why he is supporting my opponent in the election. He hopes that with a new mayor, he'll be able to build the plant without having to spend any more money."

"If I could vote, I'd vote for you, Mayor," said Polly.

"Polly, let me give you a leaflet that you and your parents might want to read. It tells about the things I believe in and about my plans for Spring Grove if I'm re-elected."

"That's a nice picture on the front, Mayor," said Ruthann.

"That's me and my wife, Betty, and our daughter, Emily. Over in the corner is a picture of our dog, Cleopatra."

"Why did you name her Cleopatra?" asked Ruthann.

"Because she belongs to a very unusual breed of dogs that came from ancient Egypt many years ago."

"Her tail is all curled up," said Polly.

"Yes, and there are other interesting things about her. Maybe some day when I have time, I'll be able to tell you more about Cleopatra. But now I have to go. It was very nice visiting with you girls, and I enjoyed my banana split, too," said the mayor.

After their meeting with the mayor, Ruthann and Polly read about the election campaign every day in the newspaper. Many of the stories seemed to be about Mr. Simpson's plant and whether it was a good idea to have it built.

Then, one day about a week before the election, the two girls were walking home from school when they saw a man passing out leaflets. On the leaflet was a picture of Mayor Waters reaching out for a thick wad of money. The man handing him the money was Mr. Simpson!

Under the picture were these words:

WATERS GETS PAID OFF TO OK SIMPSON'S PLANT!

No matter what Mayor Harmon Waters may be telling the voters of Spring Grove today, look out after the election next week! Just as soon as the election is over, Waters is going to approve the Simpson plant. That is why Simpson is handing him all that money. If you care about Spring Grove, you'll vote Mayor Harmon Waters out of office next Tuesday!

By the time that Ruthann had finished reading the story to Polly, the man handing out the leaflets had gone. Ruthann looked worried. "This is serious, Polly. The story says that Mayor Waters has taken a *bribe*. Maybe Officer Greenwood can take us to see Mr. Simpson, and we can find out what this is all about."

When the two girls got to Officer Greenwood's house, he wasn't home. "What shall we
do?" Ruthann asked Mrs. Greenwood, who had
answered the door.

"Why, come with me to see Mr. Simpson, of course," answered Gail Greenwood. "Grover isn't the only detective in this family."

Mr. Simpson lived in a big house on the edge of town. When Ruthann rang the doorbell, a butler answered. He spoke with an English accent, and he told Mrs. Greenwood and the two girls that they could not talk to Mr. Simpson.

"That's all right, Winslow, let them in," said a voice from inside the house. "I'm afraid Winslow has never really gotten used to American ways, even though he left Great Britain years ago. He still has this idea that children should be seen and not heard. But I'll talk to you girls. And to you, Mrs. Greenwood."

After they were all seated in the living room,
Ruthann said, "Mr. Simpson, we're friends of

Mayor Waters. We want to know if you really gave him money so that he would help you to get your plant built." She handed Mr. Simpson one of the leaflets. He looked at it with a smile on his face.

"Well, well," he said, "isn't that an interesting picture!"

"Mr. Simpson, will you tell us where that picture was taken?" asked Mrs. Greenwood. "It's hard to tell because the background is all fuzzy and blurred."

"It's really none of your business, but I'll tell you. Mayor Waters called me a few days ago and asked me to meet him at his home. He said he wanted to talk about the plant, and he told me to bring plenty of money."

"Did anyone see you go to the mayor's house?" asked Mrs. Greenwood.

"No. It was late at night," answered Mr. Simpson. "And I didn't want anyone to see me. I went to the front door first and rang the bell. But the mayor's dog started to bark so loudly that I thought the neighbors might hear. So I went around to the back."

"Then what happened?" asked Polly.

"Well, the mayor let me in. He told me that he didn't really care about the plant being built in Spring Grove. But he certainly did need some money. I took the hint. Someone must have been hiding outside the window with a camera. Whoever it was took a picture of me handing the money to Mayor Waters.

That picture sure won't help him in this election. If you people had any sense, you wouldn't be trying to help him, either. Now would you please leave? I'm a busy man."

"But Mr. Simpson, something you said wasn't true," said Ruthann.

"What are you talking about?" asked Mr. Simpson.

"Cleopatra!"

"Cleopatra? What kind of nonsense is that?"

"Mayor Waters' dog," said Ruthann. "She couldn't have barked like you said she did. She's a Basenji. After I saw a picture of Cleopatra, I looked her up in my dog book. Basenjis have curly tails and they come from ancient

Egypt, just like Cleopatra. And Basenjis are
the only breed of dogs that don't bark."

"Well, maybe I made a mistake about the barking . . ." said Mr. Simpson.

"You made another mistake when you had Winslow pose for that phony picture of the mayor," said Mrs. Greenwood.

"What do you mean?" shouted Mr. Simpson. "That picture is not phony!"

"Yes, it is," said Mrs. Greenwood calmly. "You had someone take a picture of you handing the money to Winslow. Then you cut Winslow's head out of the picture and pasted in Mayor Waters' head from another picture. You would have been a lot smarter if you had cut out Winslow's tie, too."

"His tie!"

"The figure in the picture has a tie with slanted stripes. But the stripes slant from the right to the left. That is the way men's ties are made in Great Britain. If you look at striped ties made in the United States, you'll see that the stripes slant from *left* to *right*. The tie in the picture came from Great Britain. I'd be willing to bet that it belongs to someone you just described. Someone who has never quite

gotten used to American habits. Someone named Winslow. In fact, if my husband came here with a search warrant, I'm sure he could find that same tie right in Winslow's closet!"

"You're an amazing person, Mrs. Greenwood. I'm afraid you've discovered the truth about my little joke," said Mr. Simpson.

"It's more than a joke, Mr. Simpson. You owe the people of Spring Grove an apology for trying to make them believe a lie. You wanted to spoil Mayor Waters' chance of being re-elected. That way you could build your plant. You can start making up for your trick right now by going down to the *Spring Grove Times* and telling the truth about what happened."

The next day, Mr. Simpson's story about the mystery of the hidden camera was published in the newspaper. The people of Spring Grove learned the truth, and when they voted in the election on Tuesday, most of them voted for Mr. Waters. The mayor won the election. A few days later, he asked Mrs. Greenwood, Ruthann, and Polly to meet him at the Ice Cream Shop.

"You three are responsible for my re-election," Mayor Waters said. "But more important than that, Mr. Simpson has agreed to put the pollution control equipment into his new plant. Now it can be built *safely*. We all owe you our thanks. Polly and Ruthann, may I treat you to some ice cream?"

"Banana splits!" said Ruthann and Polly together.

"Mrs. Greenwood, would you like something?" asked the mayor.

"I don't see why not. You can make mine a banana split, too," said Mrs. Greenwood.

"I understand that's also Grover's favorite," said the mayor.

"That's right," answered Mrs. Greenwood.

"I'm beginning to think that the secret of being a good detective is to eat banana splits."

"There must be more to it than that," said Mayor Waters. "But there's one thing I still don't understand about the detective work you did on Mr. Simpson's case. How on earth do you know so much about the patterns of men's neckties?"

"You may not believe it, Mr. Mayor," said Mrs. Greenwood, "but I read about it in a mystery story!"